Olde New Englai
STRANGE SUPERST

This book is dedicated to my niece and godchild, Cheryl Cahill of Beverly, Massachusetts. She is filled with superstitions, most of them quaint. They have become an integral part of her personality, so I hope they never leave her.

Accused witch Sarah Good awaits execution at Gallows Hill, Salem - 1692. With the noose firmly around her neck, the hooded hangman will push her off the ladder. Thus originated the superstition that walking under a ladder brings bad luck—one might be struck by a falling witch!

Photo by Mikki Ansin, from the television production, "Three Sovereigns For Sarah," courtesy Nightowl Productions, Nahant, MA.

©Copyright, Old Saltbox, 1990 ISBN: 0-9626162-0-6

Cover Photo:
Illustration by famed artist Howard Pyle; photo and coloring by Steve Harwood.

INTRODUCTION

Each generation that comes along seems to consider itself less superstitious than the one that preceded it. In Pilgrim and Puritan days their belief in the devil and his disciple, the witch, was so intense that it turned their world upside down. In the early 1700's, New Englanders were embarrassed by the fanatical beliefs of their forefathers, and a popular poem often recited in the streets of Boston was: *"In Superstition's days 'tis said, hens laid two eggs on Monday; Because a hen would loose her head, that laid an egg on Sunday. Now our wise rulers and the law, say none shall wash on Sunday; So Boston folks must dirty go, and wash then twice on Monday."* Although the witchcraft days had ended, strange superstitions persisted well into the next century, as Sarah Emery of Newburyport revealed in 1785: *"In every community,"* she wrote, *"there was one or more believed to possess an 'evil eye,' and in every house could be seen horse shoes above the doors, and other charms against their machinations."* One hundred years later, Samuel Adams Drake wrote: *"It is a question whether there are not as many popular superstitions today among plain New England country-folk as at any time since the settlement of the country. The belief in the virtue of the horseshoe is unabated."* It seems then, that well into the 19th century, our ancestors were a superstitious lot.

My mother, born at the turn of the 20th century, was especially superstitious and wary of the doings of the devil, but my common-sense father, who often critisized my mother for her unfounded fears, was forever knocking on wood and avoiding black cats. He, however, did not consider himself to be superstitious. I think that I am much less superstitious than my parents were; yet, I sometimes find myself following their examples, doing nonsensible things for good luck and not doing certain things, like walking under a ladder, because it might bring me bad luck. I do believe that there is a good spiritual force at work in this world, and if you believe as I do, then we must take our thinking one step further—that there must be an evil force at work here too. If that's true, then our thinking can't be very different today than that of the Pilgrims and Puritans. And their beliefs got them into a lot of trouble!

Bob Cahill

The 1693 cover of one of Cotton Mather's many books on devils and witchcraft, which he titled, "The Wonders of the Invisible World." Below is the illustration used in John Milton's "Paradise Lost," published in 1688, depicting the devil stirring up the fiery pit filled with suffering sinners.

I
Raising The Devil

The devil today is considered a joke, and most people don't believe he exists—yet, there are some sixty passages in the Bible referring to Satan and his works. Jesus, who was tempted by the devil for forty days in the wilderness, calls him, *"the father of lies,"* and supposedly the devil is still with us and leads us into temptation on a daily basis. Famous comedian Red Skelton's favorite line when caught in some mischievous prank was always, *"the devil made me do it."* And thus was the sincere belief of our ancestors—if you weren't fully in God's graces in all your thoughts and activities, the devil would make you do evil things. *"He who believes in the devil,"* wrote Thomas Mann, *"already belongs to him."* And New England's first settlers of Pilgrims and Puritans were firmly convinced that Satan was alive and well and living among them.

"This is the devil's territory," cried Cotton Mather, the leading Puritan minister of the late 17th century, from his pulpit in Boston. *"The Devil's Army is horribly broke in upon us,"* he said during the witch-hysteria of 1692, *"at Salem, which is the center, and after a sort, the first born of our English settlements."* This unshakable belief that an unseen and evil force was in their midst, not only heightened their fears in this new wild world, but aggravated the bizarre superstitions already implanted in their minds when they arrived here from Europe.

Even two centuries after their arrival, New Englanders were steeped in superstitions, still stimulated by the devil's army of demons, ever-present at every level of society. *"My native town of Marblehead, like other fishing towns,"* wrote United States Supreme Court Justice Joseph Story in the mid 1800's, *"as I believe, was full of all sorts of superstitions. Ghosts, hobgoblins, will-o-whisps, apparitions, and premonitions, were the common, I might almost say, the universal subject of belief, and numberless were the stories of haunted houses and wandering spirits, and murdered ghosts, that were told at the fireside, and filled my imagination with every kind of preternatural fear."* The second President of The United States, John Adams, also commented on the subject, by saying, *"If the ancients drank wine as New Englanders drink rum and cider, it is no wonder we hear of so many possessed with devils."* John Adams, in fact, before he became President, helped to squelch a grizzly superstition that was once the law of the land:

John Ames of Boxford, Massachusetts had been accused of murdering his wife Ruth in 1769. She had been found dead in their home by John's mother, and the doctor concluded that Ruth had been poisoned. Brought to court at Salem, the Magistrates decided that John should undergo the *"Ordeal of Touch."* Also known as *"Bier Right,"* it was believed that a corpse would bleed when touched by the murderer. If the body did not bleed, the accused was innocent. John Adams, the attorney representing John Ames, refused to allow his client to touch the body of his wife, which preplexed the judges and jury, for there seemed to be no other way to determine the guilt or innocence of the accused. *"This is nothing but black-arts and witchcraft,"* John Adams shouted at the Magistrates, and thus, he won the case and John Ames was allowed to go free. To my knowledge, the Ordeal of Touch was never again suggested in a court of law in New England. Coincidently, however, 77 years prior to this murder trial at the Salem courthouse, Rebecca Ames, John Ames' grandmother, was found guilty of witchcraft. The Captain of the Jury that condemned her was Thomas Perley, grandfather to Ruth Perley Ames, John's supposedly murdered wife—so maybe there was *"black-arts and witchcraft"* involved here, or belated revenge, and the future President of The United States was instrumental in allowing a murderer to be set free.

One wonders in retrospect, was it God or the devil that made the victim bleed when touched by the guilty party, for in the minds of our forefathers, it had to be one or the other that performed these supernatural acts. Even common natural occurences like thunder and lightning were often considered acts of God's wrath, and at other times, the devil's doings. Average citizens didn't know who was playing havoc with them, until the local minister explained it as either a good or evil occurence. And of course, the minister was never quite sure either. The common rationale for the clergy was that God, angry over sins committed by members of the flock, showed His discontent by providing a disaster such as an earthquake or hurricane. God also displayed His wrath on individuals, the clergy insisted. Governor John Winthrop, in his 1630s Journal, writes, *"this woman died in great dispair,"* (after her new-born baby had expired) *"and she was trembling so as it shook the room, and crying out her torment, saying now she must go to everlasting torments."* The local minister had convinced her that God had taken her baby because of her previous sins. Governor Winthrop also writes that in 1637 another woman, *"with troubled mind about her spiritual estate, grew into utter desperation and could not endure to hear of any comfort. So, one day she took her little infant and threw it into a well and then came into the house and said, now she was sure she should be damned, for she had drowned her child."*

A year later at Salmon Falls, Massachusetts, Mary Hortado, who was constantly being accused of *"Sabbath-breaking,"* told the local minister that she didn't have to go to Sunday meetings for God came to visit her at home.

Soon afterwards, her home began to creak and moan and some timbers fell, almost hitting her on the head. The minister and other villagers concluded that the devil was now her constant visitor because she had lied. Mary, obviously a spunky and fearless woman, layed bay branches around inside and outside her house, a sure cure for getting rid of the devil and his demons. Apparently the devil didn't like the sweet smell, for town records reveal, *"As long as the branches continued to green, there was quiet in the house."* Mary Hortado, although later accused and acquitted of witchcraft, wasn't one to be intimidated by the devil, or by the local minister.

Leading ministers of all the Puritan towns and villages of New England, sometimes gathered together in an attempt to unify and justify their teachings and to swap stories of the devil and Doomsday. Such meetings were probably a main stimulus for the 1692 witch-hysteria at Salem. As noted historian Chadwick Hansen wrote, *"The clergy may have stimulated the community into mass hysterics, attributable to some narrowness or fanaticism or repressiveness peculiar to Puritans."* At one of these meetings of Puritan ministers at Cambridge, Massachusetts, a harmless garden-snake wiggled across the meetinghouse floor. The black-frocked clergymen panicked and raced for the door, as Deacon Thomas of Braintree, braver than the others, stomped it with his foot, squashing its head. The snake, a symbol of the devil since the days of Adam and Eve, completely disrupted their meeting, and all present agreed that the snake was *"the devil, attempting to disturb and dissolution us."* It was a disfigured calf that interrupted a meeting at Ipswich in 1646. The calf was *"brought forth to the meetinghouse,"* writes Governor Winthrop, *"for all to see."* He described it as having *"three noses and six eyes...and it meant an evil sign."*

Cotton Mather's father, Reverend Increase Mather, President of Harvard College, and also a leading religious spokesman in New England, decried superstitions as *"unlawful"* and in a second breath, called them, *"the devil's work."* Many that he mentioned as against Puritan law, included: *"horseshoes nailed over doors, placing urine in a bottle to expel diseases, spells and charms, herbs and plants to preserve from witchcraft, and drawing blood from those whom they suspect as witches."* Increase Mather assured his fellow ministers and citizens of New England that, *"these superstitions do work, but they are from Satan."* He considered himself an expert on many subjects, including witches, ghosts and comets, but especially the devil and his works. In 1682, he asked all the ministers of New England to send him *"wonder stories,"* be they works of good or evil, so that he could write his, *"Essay For The Recording of Illustrious Providences."* This book of amazing events was compiled not only for his friends in England and Ireland, but for the local populace as well. The *"wonders"* accumulated by Mather included stories of earthquakes, comets, appearances of ghosts, animal phenomena, occult happenings and human birth of monsters.

An order to all village and town leaders from the Governor and his Council in 1647, decreed that every community of over fifty people must *"appoint one within their Towne to teach all children as shall resort to him to write and read.... It being one chief project of that old deluder Satan, to keep men from the knowledge of the Scriptures."* Therefore, when Mather's *"Essay"* was printed and available in the 1680's, there were many local readers, hungry for the supernatural and often diabolical stories he presented. There was other reading matter available to Puritans at that time as well: Nathaniel Crouch's *"Delights For The Ingenious,"* on fortune-telling; John Josselyn's *"New England Rareties,"* on local superstitions and Indian legends; Samuel Danforth's *"Almanac"* "on astrology and prophecies; and Samuel Willard's *"The Fiery Tryal,"* on mystical monsters and spirits, to name only a few. These books were what our Puritan ancestors were absorbing, making them even more fearful and paranoid than they already were.

In one of his discourses on comets, Increase Mather wrote. *"It is common observation, verified by the experience of many ages, that great and public calamities seldom come upon any place without prodigious warnings to forerun and signify what is to be expected....Comets are portentous and signal of great and notable changes."* Another noted scholar of Increase Mather's time, was Simon Bradstreet, Govenor of the Bay Colony from 1679 to 1686. He also believed that comets were forewarnings of disasters. *"The star of 1664,"* he wrote *"caused a great and dreadful plague that followed the next Summer, in a dreadful war by sea with the Dutch, and the burning of London the second year following."* His son, John Bradstreet of Rowley was arrested and tried at Salem in 1652, *"for having familiarity with the devil."* In court he admitted that he *"read a book of magic and heard a voice asking what work I had for him,"* meaning that he had used magic to get the devil to talk to him. Bradstreet testified under oath, *"I asked the devil to make a bridge of sand over the sea, and make a ladder of sand to heaven, then go to God and come to me no more."* The Magistrates found John only guilty of lying and ordered him to be fined and whipped. He found himself in another dilemma in 1692, however, when he was accused of witchcraft. He was indicted for *"inciting a dog to afflict others,"* which could mean a death sentence during Witch Times. John ran away and hid in the woods, thus avoiding the hangman, but the dog he incited to give two teenaged girls *"the evil eye,"* was hanged. John's brother Dudley was a magistrate at Andover and immersed in the witch delusion as well. He had already presented forty warrants for constables to arrest people accused of witchcraft, when he became disgusted with the entire procedure and refused to issue anymore warrants. His fellow townsfolk then accused him of witchcraft; so, leaving his belongings, he and his wife, like his brother before him, fled town. Govenor Bradstreet, although a religious man who bragged that he had read the Bible through before he was seven years old, had also read books on the occult and had dabbled in fortune-telling. His interests were pursued by his offspring, and all, father and sons, suffered gravely for their interest in the supernatural.

"There shall not be found among you anyone who... uses divination, one who practices witchcraft, or one who interprets omens..." reads the Bible in Deuteronomy, Chapter 18, verse 10. Yet, the leaders of Puritan society in the 1600's were executing those who they thought were practicing witchcraft, while they, the Mathers, Winthrops and Bradstreets, were *"interpreting omens,"* such as comets as prodigious warnings. When Quakers began arriving in New England in 1635, they accused the Puritans of following *"Pagan superstitions,"* as Ann Hutchinson, a leading Quaker called it. The Puritan leaders didn't like the criticisms, and they banned most Quakers from the Colony, or hanged them. The Pilgrims of Plymouth were just as harsh on Quakers, and many Pilgrims turned Quaker were forced out of Plymouth to the sandy barren soil of Cape Cod. The Quakers, however, also believed in some of the old-world superstitions, although theirs seemed more quaint and harmless than those of the Puritans.

One belief among Quakers was that mice will leave a house just before there is a death in it, and that rats will leave a dock in premonition that a ship about to depart will never return. Rodents and not humans, according to 17th century Quakers, were the devil's disciples. Humans could only be tempted by the devil, but rats often carried his venomous messages of lies and deceit. To rid a house or a ship of rats, believed the Quakers, one had to write to them with warnings and threats of death and leave the letter where they would find it. Only harsh words on paper would force the rats to leave the premises. One such letter exorcising rats from a Quaker home was found in the mid-1800's in a crevice of a crumbling cellar-hole wall at Sandwich on Cape Cod. It was discovered by the great-great-grand niece of Emmy Weed, the writer of the letter, and it was addressed to the rats of the house. It read as follows:

"I have been with you till my patience is all gone. I cannot find words bad enough to express what I feel, you black devils. You are gnawing our tracecorn while we are asleep! And when we are awake, you have the audacity to set your infernal jaws to going. Now, spirits of the bottomless pit, depart from this place with all speed! Look not back! Begone, or you are ruined! We are preparing water to drown you; fire to roast you; cats to catch you; and clubs to maul you. Quit here and go to Ike Nute's. A hint to the wise

is sufficient. To the biggest and most inventive rat. Mrs. Weed."

The reason why the letter survived almost two centuries in the damp cellar is because the paper was made of linen and was covered by a second blank piece of paper. Unfortunately for Emmy Weed, the letter probably didn't work, for in bygone days most everyone knew that the rats must eat the letter in order to understand the contents.

One superstition that Puritans, Pilgrims and Quakers all agreed on, was the righteous spiritual intervention in the *"Trial-By-Ordeal."* It was sanctioned by many New England communities well up until the days of the Revolutionary War. If a person was thought to be a thief, but there was no substantial evidence of his thievery, the Trial-By-Ordeal was often evoked. The accused was made to thrust hand and arm, usually up to the elbow, into a pot of boiling water. After a second or two, he took his arm out and it was immediately bandaged. When the bandage was removed a few days later, if there were burns on his arm and hand, he was guilty of theft, but if there were no burn marks, he was innocent of any crime. It worked basically on the same principal as the Ordeal-of-Touch, when supernatural spirits were prevailed upon to decide the fate of an individual. Many times the Trial-By-Ordeal was decided by a fist-fight or wrestling match. Coincidentally, when the White man came to this land, he found the Indians used similar methods of combat to decide guilt or innocence—the Great Spirit saw to it that righteousness prevailed, and in the White man's world, God would intervene and truth would win out.

In Connecticut, where the towns of Old Lyme and New London met, the settlers decided on Trial-By-Ordeal as a way to solve a boundary dispute. Each group chose their strongest man, and the two men met each other in combat on the disputed land. It was America's first official bareknuckles fist-fight. The fight lasted for over five hours with much betting transpiring between the two sides. At last, *"the Lord made his decision,"* and Matthew Griswold of Old Lyme knocked out his New London opponent. Old Lyme officially claimed the disputed boundary land which it holds to this day. But, as New Londoners are quick to point out, God later gave New London America's first Navy.

The sailors of America's first Navy, much like the men of the sea before them, began to concoct their own bevy of superstitions and traditions during the Revolutionary War. British tars and New England merchant mariners were even more wary of the supernatural than their landlubbing counterparts, and as historian Samuel Adams Drake wrote, *"New England was the child of a superstitious mother."* Venturing forth to brave the unknown over unpredictable seas and visiting strange mysterious lands, made

17th and 18th century sailors especially attuned to good and bad omens—and they seemed to give the devil more respect than those who found their occupations on land. Herman Melville wrote *"that in maritime life, far more than in that of terra-firma, wild rumors abound, wherever there is any adequate reality for them to cling to."* Ministers, or any other holy man for that matter, whenever possible, were not allowed to board vessels for fear their presence on deck might stir the wrath of the devil, who in turn, could make long voyages difficult ones. Women were also kept from boarding ships because they were a bad omen. Many sailors honestly feared for their lives if a woman was allowed to join them on a voyage, yet vessels were and are still referred to as *"her"* and *"she,"* even if the vessel has a masculine name. This has been true since ancient times when vessels were thought to be protected by pagan goddesses, with the image of the goddess painted or sculpted on the bow. This practice evolved into the carving of figureheads for all large sailing ships, as did the superstition that sculptured wooden figureheads protected the vessel and her occupants.

At about the turn of the 19th century in Salem, wealthy ship-owner Stephen Phillips hired carpenter Joe True to carve the bust of the Apostle Paul for the bow of his ship, SAINT PAUL. This vessel bacame a successful cargo carrier for Phillips and she traveled the world for some twelve years without a mishap. Returning to home port after a long voyage, the bust of Saint Paul was removed for repairs, and a few days later the SAINT PAUL headed out to sea again with a cargo bound for Manila. When they were only a few miles out of Salem the crew noticed that the figurehead was missing. Many begged the captain to turn the vessel around to retrieve it, but he refused, leaving the crew with the jitters and rumblings among themselves that the vessel was surely doomed without her figurehead. At the first port-of-call, second mate Jack Hancock told the captain that he refused to reboard the SAINT PAUL after taking his shore leave. Even if it meant he could never ship out again on another vessel, he informed the captain that he would not sail aboard the SAINT PAUL without her protective bust of the apostle fastened to the prow. The ship sailed without him, and unfortunately for all aboard, Jack Hancock's premonitition proved to be right. The SAINT PAUL and her occupants were never seen again.

The christening of a vessel with a bottle of champagne smashed over the bow also harkens back to pagan superstition. The ancients set up an altar at the bow and poured wine and oil over it, seeking protection from goddesses of the sea. The Vikings went one step further and offered the gods and goddesses human blood, crushing a man as a human sacrifice under the log-rollers that sent the vessel down the ways and to sea. In New England, the opposite was believed by sailors—if anyone was killed or injured during the launching of a vessel, the vessel became a hoodoo ship, and crewmen usually refused to sail on her. The term *"christening"* for the ceremony prior to launching, came when Europeans converted from pagan gods and goddesses to Christianity, but the procedures and ceremony remain with champagne replacing the wine, oil, and blood.

New England sailors also believed that anyone with red hair aboard ship could be bad luck for that ship. Redheaded women were an especial taboo. Although the devil was often depicted by Puritan New Englanders as being a black man, or appearing as a man dressed in black, the ancients usually described him as being red, or dressed in red. The evil gods of China and Egypt were colored red, and pagan legend reveals that the devil had red hair. Some of this prejudice against redheads also comes from English history, when feared Viking and Celts invaded England, many of their warriors having red hair. Puritan doctors in New England often diagnosed redheaded or red-faced persons as being *"sinners with bad blood."* And Judas Iscariot, so claimed Puritan ministers, was a redhead.

A redheaded woman named Sarah Reynolds was banned by law from the settlement at the Isles of Shoals, New Hampshire in 1647. Defying the court order that prohibited women from living at the Isles, she set up housekeeping with her husband John, and her red hair only further infuriated the superstitious fishermen who lived there. Fisherman Richard Cutt petitioned the court to have her removed, *"together with the hogs and swine running at large on the island."* Although she had two strikes against her, the landlubbing Magistrates allowed Sarah to remain at the Isles, but *"only during good behavior"*—apparently Sarah had a temper to match her hair. As recently as 1986, there was a court dispute regarding this superstition in Ireland, when a young redheaded woman named Ellen O'Connor was refused a ride on a ferry-barge near Galway. The ferry-master considered her *"a Jonah,"* because of her red hair and wouldn't let her board. The fiery redhead took the old ferry-master to court and won passage, six months later.

Webster's Dictionary describes a Jonah, not only as the Hebrew prophet who was swallowed by a whale, but as *"a person who brings bad luck, especially on board a ship."* Not just redheads were Jonahs, but men who were missing a limb or had some malady or disfigurement. An old salty saying was that, *"A man who has been chewed by a shark is a Jonah, for all who sail with him know that if he goes back to sea, that shark is going to get the rest of him."* Also, if a shark constantly followed a vessel, it was believed that a man aboard would soon die. If a man aboard was thought to be a Jonah, he was often set adrift in an open-boat or was dropped off on a desolate island. Many sailors considered this perfectly justifiable to protect themselves against the workings of the devil. The Jonah at sea, like the witch on land, was the devil's disciple, and one could go to any lengths to interrupt the devil's evil intentions.

To name a vessel JONAH was, according to seamen, only asking for trouble, but a ship of that name sailed from France to the Americas in 1612. Aboard were French colonists and Catholic priests on their way to Canada to become Indian missionaries. After getting lost in a fog, the JONAH landed at Mount Desert Island, now Bar Harbor, Maine. The Jesuit fathers decided that the thick fog, being lifted to reveal the island, was divine intervention—so they and some of the colonists settled there, immediately constructing a church, the Mission of Saint Sauveur. A few months later, Englishman Samuel Argall and a crew from Jamestown, Virginia, also landed at Mount Desert Island. Although the French offered no resistance, many were massacred, some were set adrift in rowboats, and a few were brought back to Virginia as slaves. No Catholic priests knowingly set foot on New England soil for almost two centuries after that episode, and to my knowledge, no sailing ship named JONAH has ever ventured into New England waters since.

"Every ship reached New England safely but the ANGEL GABRIEL," wrote William Hibbens of Boston in 1642, which, to the first settlers, was an evil omen. The Puritans blamed the disappearence at sea of the ANGEL GABRIEL on her compass, for the compass was considered *"an instrument of the devil."* Only evil magic could cause a needle in fluid to point to magnetic-north, and sailors were always wary or it. Although navigators made many errors in reading compasses, or nearby metal objects disrupted and changed the readings setting ships off course, the devil was invariably the culprit responsible for shipwrecks and sinkings. It was Nathaniel Bowditch of Salem, in the mid 1800's, who taught many sailors how to navigate by the stars, sextant and compass, dispelling salty old superstitions about the compass being the devil's instrument. Bowditch's book on navigation is still being used to this day, and next to the Bible, has sold more copies than any other book ever written. Prior to the compass, pigs were thought to be the most trustworthy navigational aids at sea. Live pigs were often aboard to afford the crew fresh meat on long voyages, but when the ship was lost at sea, one of the pigs was thrown overboard. Sailors believed that pigs, by instinct, would always swim toward the nearest land even though they couldn't see it. Once the pig was in the ocean, the man at the helm would sail the ship in whatever direction the pig started swimming.

Besides being shipwrecked or lost at sea, another dread for sailors was being becalmed for long periods of time, unable to catch enough wind to fill the ship's sails. One way to call up the wind, sailors believed and practiced, was to stick a knife into the mainmast in the direction they wanted the wind to blow. But their greatest taboo was to *"whistle for a breeze"* when becalmed, for that would enrage the devil into providing a tempest. The only whistle allowed aboard a sailing ship was the boatswain's whistle that called the crew on deck. Any other kind of whistling aboard ship usually meant a flogging for the guilty crewman. Yankee sailors wouldn't allow umbrellas aboard for they were bad luck, and this is still a tradition in the United States Navy. Another is that, if a hatch is accidentally or purposely turned upside-down, it will bring a curse to the vessel and her crew. If there is a death aboard a ship, the body is soon disposed of in the sea, but the spirit of the man, it is still believed in many quarters, remains aboard and will in some way warn remaining crew members of impending danger. Any sailor today will tell you that it's bad luck for a ship to leave port on a Friday, but good luck to leave on a voyage on Sunday, based on the old saying *"Sunday sail, never fails; Friday sail, bad luck and gales"*. A rainbow seen from the deck is considered a good luck omen, unless it's seen just before the sun goes down, then it's a bad omen. This coincides with the popular saying, often quoted by seamen today, *"Red sky in the morning, sailors take warning. Red sky at night, sailors delight."* Birds and bees are considered good luck if they land on a vessel, with the exception of crows, blackbirds, owls and hawks. To shoot a bird that lands on a ship is considered a terrible offense and a sure sign of impending doom to the crew. In *"The Ancient Mariner,"* by Samuel Coleridge, a large albatross that was following a ship is deliberately shot, and all aboard suffer the consequences. The clumsy, webb-footed albatross contains the soul of a drowned sailor, so our forefathers believed, and its presence on or near a vessel was a divine omen.

John Josselyn crossed the Atlantic to visit New England for the second time in 1663, and while off the New Hampshire coast he recorded the following strange incident: *"A flame settled upon the main mast,"* he wrote, *"at about eight in the evening. It was about the bigness of a great candle and is called by our seamen, Saint Elmo's Fire. It comes before a storm, and is commonly thought to be a Spirit."* Men of every seafaring country had varying beliefs concerning Saint Elmo's Fire, but all agreed that it was either a good or bad omen. These eerie lights appear on mastheads, rigging, bowsprit and booms of sailing ships, usually before or during a storm, and in bygone days it often frightened those who witnessed it dancing about a vessel. Some thought this sparking fire was the devil himself, whereas others accepted the lights in awe as a visitation from angels assuring them that neither they nor the ship were in any danger. Celtic fishermen from Brittany who fished the waters just north of New England almost a century before the Pilgrims arrived here, believed Saint Elmo's Fire was a blessed message from heaven assuring them that their vessel would not sink and no member of the crew would drown. The Portuguese fishermen from Gloucester, Massachusetts, call this phenomenon, *"Corpo Santo,"* meaning *"the Saint's body,"* and they also believe to this day that its appearance predicts salvation of ship and crew in a storm. Saint Elmo's Fire is sparks of electricity attracted to iron fittings on the ship, nothing more, but to some seamen it was miraculous and to others, a menacing message from the devil.

Another natural phenomenon that evoked high anxiety in superstitious seamen, was the *"cawl"* or *"veil,"* an extra layer of skin or membrane that sometimes envelopes the faces of newborn babies. An old Scots and Irish belief was that a baby born with a cawl was gifted, could see spirits, and throughout his or her life would be able to predict future events, but most important to seamen was the belief that anyone born with a veil could never drown. Many captains and crews would not leave port unless a cawl from a recently born baby was aboard the ship they were to be sailing on. Cawls were often traded from one vessel to another, as one ship came home and another sailed off to distant lands. Having a cawl aboard was a guarantee that the ship wouldn't sink, and they were often sold to sea captains and shipowners for large sums of money. Even on land, the cawl and those born with a cawl were highly respected. It was said of the great gunfighter of America's wild west, Staka Lee, that he was greatly feared because, *"he was born with a veil over his face, and everybody knows that babies born with veils on their faces kin see ghosts and raise 41 kinds of hell."*

That thoughts of hell and fear of the devil were ever present, not only at sea but along the seacoast of New England, is further evidenced in some of the names the Pilgrims and Puritans gave to places where the devil's works had supposedly been performed and sometimes witnessed. Even the kelp that attaches itself to tidal-rocks and often drifts ashore is still called *"the devil's apron."* At Peabody, Massachusetts, once called Salem Farms, where those accused of witchcraft lived in 1692, there is a pond called *"The Devil's Dishfull,"* and at nearby Marblehead, offshore is an island called *"Satan Rock."* At Newport, Rhode Island there is *"The Devil's Seat,"* which Cotton Mather tells us, *"is at the very edge of a precipice where, with his tail laid over his shoulder as a scepter, the devil would majestically direct the exercises."* Located in Millington, Connecticut, at Chapman Falls, is *"The Devil's Hopyard,"* where, Samuel Adams Drake said, *"old witches meet on stormy nights to make potions."* There is *"Devil's Bridge"* off Martha's Vineyard, where many great vessels have met disaster. And off Cape Cod there is *"The Devil's Pillow,"* and the *"Devil's Leap,"* and the *"Devil's Ash Heap,"* the latter being a name Martha's Vineyard people sometimes give to Nantucket Island. There are hundreds of locations throughout New England that have the

"Devil" as a prefix, all connected by some old legend or disaster that was believed to be perpetrated by the evil one.

At a small body of water once called *"Devil's Pond"* by the inhabitants of Windsor, Connecticut, there was an uproar of evil in the Spring of 1758. Unseen demons began to growl and scream from the pond in the middle of the night, waking all in the village. They sprang from their beds, and in panic, ran from their homes and into the woods away from the pond. At dawn the frightening sounds subsided and the sleepless villagers gingerly returned to their homes. A few of the braver residents ventured to the banks of the pond, their muskets at the ready. They sheepishly returned to the village a few minutes later to report that the fiendish cries they heard in the night were not from the devil and his coven of demons, but from a bevy of mating bullfrogs.

II
Wisdom of the Witches

"When I came to the sight of where John Procter did live, there was a hard blow struck to my breast, which caused great pain in my stomach, and amazement in my head. Afterwards, about half a mile from the house, I was taken speechless for some short time. And when we came to the way where Salem Road goeth into Ipswich Road, there I received another blow on my breast which caused much pain, and I could not sit on my horse. . . . After I came home again to Newbury, I was pinched and nipped by something invisible for some time." These were the words of Joseph Bailey recorded in Salem court in 1692, known as the Witch Times. John Procter and his wife Elizabeth were soon after arrested for *"sundry acts of witchcraft,"* and both were later hanged at Gallows Hill in Salem, Massachusetts. It is obvious today that Mr. Bailey, knowing he was passing the home of suspected witches, suffered a mild heart attack or anxiety pains due to his fears, and the nipping and pinching he experienced at home were probably from horse-fleas.

"A ride through the woods then (during Witch Times) *was little coveted by the stoutest hearts,"* historian Samuel Adams Drake tells us. *"A spark of fear is soon blown into uncontrollable panic. Bushes grow spectres and trees outstretched goblin arms."* Elizabeth Hubbard, one of the witch accusers of Salem, Drake writes *"was riding home from meeting on the crupper, behind old Clement Coldum. The rustling leaves were witches' whisperings, the white birches seemed ghosts in their winding-sheets. The woman, faint-hearted and overmastered by a nameless dread, cried out to the goodman to ride for life—the woods were full of devils."* The devil and his disciples were everywhere in Essex County, but especially in Salem, the shire town, and in neighboring villages.

Under the first code of New England's Puritan colonies passed in 1641, witchcraft was one of twelve crimes punishable by death. The article read: *"If any man or woman be a witch, that is, hath consulted with a familiar spirit, he or she shall be put to death."* Cotton Mather described witchcraft as, *"the doing of strange and, for the most part, ill things by the help of evil spirits."* And these *"familiars"* and *"evil spirits"* were considered either invisible or able to change their form and size at will, which made them all the more frightening. The devil, so it was believed, provided each witch with an impish, beastly familiar which could appear as a common cat, dog, bird, or other animal that would gain its sustenance by sucking on a witch's wart or pimple. To become a witch one not only had to have sexual relations with the devil and sign his book as a disciple, but it was implied that the witch had to have sexual relations with her familiar as well.

Rebecca Greensmith of Hartford, Connecticut, confessed to being a witch in 1662. *"I had familiarity with the devil,"* she testified before the Magistrates. Increase Mather recorded, *"Mother Greensmith said that the devil first appeared to her as a deer... and at last would talk to her. Moreover, she said that the devil had frequently carnal knowledge of her body."* Rebecca said *"I liked it very much,"* and on this testimony she was hanged the following year. Twenty years later, Dorothy Duent brought her child's babysitter to court, testifying that she caught the old woman, Amy Duny, *"trying to suckle my child."* Amy Duny was imprisoned, and the baby, believed cursed because it was suckled by a witch, was taken to Doctor Jacob, who was considered an expert at breaking the spell of a witch. Jacob's solution was to wrap the baby in a blanket and hang it in the fireplace. The heat of the fire would cause the witch's familiar to fall out of the blanket. Mrs. Duent followed the instructions, and as the baby wriggled and screamed in the chimney, *"a toad fell out and into the fire. It burned quickly with a flashing in the fire like gunpowder."* The baby had slight burn marks on its legs but was no longer cursed. Nothing more was reported on poor old Amy Duny.

Four Connecticut women were executed as witches in 1647, only six years after the death penalty was adopted. The first was Alice, also known as Achsah Young. Her real crime was knowledge of curing herbs, much of it obtained from local Indians and European gardeners of Essex, England, and Holland. Her magical cures of various diseases led her to the gallows. Following close behind to meet the hangman was Mary Johnson of Wethersfield. She confessed in court *"the devil appears to me and lays with me, and clears my hearth of ashes."* According to Governor Hutchinson's Essay of 1718, Mary also told the Magistrates *"the devil hunts hogs out of my cornfield, and I could not forbear laughing to see how he seized them about."*

The following year, Margaret Jones of Charlestown, Massachusetts was dragged into court. She was a noted witch-doctor in her home town and in neighboring Boston. Even the Mathers had visited her to gain knowledge of various cures from her herb garden. She was stripped naked and her body searched for *"the devil's mark"*—a wart or mole where the familiar drank its bloody-milk. *"In a hidden place she was found to have a witch's mark,"* reported John Winthrop, the Governor of Massachusetts, *"a teat, as fresh as if newly sucked."* Margaret Jones was hanged at the Frog-pond on Boston Common. In the court record-book it says that she was found guilty of *"having and using the Malignant touch."* The evil touch of a witch was often the cause of spreading diseases, so thought 17th century New Englanders. If a witch touched you, she and the devil could do with you what they wished, and you had no power left in you to resist. A hostile look or glare from a witch could also place you under her spell. During the Salem hysteria, Cotton Mather reported *"Bridget Bishop did place her evil eye on the girls, so that they were presently struck down."* When Doctor William Griggs of Salem Village first witnessed the girls taking fits in their homes, he concluded that, *"the evil hand is upon them."*

Molly Ellis, known as the *"Witch of Plymouth,"* complained that the cows owned by her neighbor, Farmer Stevens, were grazing upon her land. Stevens paid no attention to her complaint, so Molly took it upon herself to go out into the pasture and stare down each cow and curse them all. Stevens witnessed this, and thought little of it, until his cows got sick and three of them died within three years. After his third cow keeled over, Stevens marched over to Molly Ellis' house and stormed right into her bedroom without knocking. *"And there she lay on her back in bed, a-chewin and a-mutterin dretful spell words,"* Stevens reported. William Bliss writes that, *"Old Moll was dretful scart of Stevens, and promised she'd never harm him or his cows again, But, when she was talking, a little black devil, that looked just like a bumblebee, flew into the window and popped down her throat: t'was the one she had sent out to scare the cattle and horses."*

Another neighborly dispute in April of 1692 at Salem, set John Louder against the outspoken witch Bridget Bishop. *"Her chickens were coming into my garden,"* he complained to the magistrates, *" and some little time afterwards, about the dead of night, I felt a great weight upon my breast. I awakened and did clearly see said Bridget Bishop, or her likeness, sitting upon my stomach. She presently laid hold of my throat and almost choked me, and I had no strength or power in my hands to resist to help myself. In this condition, she held me to almost day."* Louder went on to testify, *"some time after that... I did see a black thing jump into the window, and it came and stood before my face. The body of it looked like a monkey, only the feet were like cock's feet with claws, and the face somewhat more like a man's than a monkey's... Upon which I cried out... and so it sprung back and flew out over the apple trees, flinging the dust with its feet. It also shook many apples off from the tree."* Bridget's familiar seems to be the most imaginative of the lot, and surely sent chills up and down spines of those in the courthouse when Louder told this fantastic story. His testimony and that of other neighbors was enough to send Bridget to the gallows, the first of 19 to be hanged at Salem in 1692.

The familiars most in vogue in the 1600's seemed to be cats, especially black cats, yet in ancient times when Paganism and witchcraft prevailed, black cats were not only considered lucky but sacred as well. The Egyptians believed that if a black cat nudged you and purred, you would be protected by the gods for a year; but if you hurt or accidentally killed a black cat, you were executed. Many mumified black cats have been uncovered in the ancient tombs of Egypt. In Middle Ages, however, black cats were considered evil. It was thought that witches transformed themselves into cats, and in France, Germany, Scotland, and England, they were burned along with the witches by the sackfulls. The French and the French-Canadians believed that a witch, called *"Loup-Garou,"* was allowed by the devil to turn into a cat at will, but in order to take human form again, she had to drink the blood of a holy person. The Egyptians believed that a cat had nine lives. But it was the French who insisted that you will have bad luck if a black cat crosses your path, a superstition that is still with us today.

New Hampshire's first witch, Jane Walford, was known by her neighbors in Hampton and Portsmouth as *"the Cat Woman,"* and in April of 1656 she was brought to trial for practicing witchcraft. A Mrs. Trimmings testified against her, stating that she met Jane in the woods one day at Hampton *"and she asked me to lend her a pound of cotton. I told her I had but two pounds and would not spare any. She then left me, and I was struck as with a clap of fire on the back, and she vanished toward the waterside in the shape of a cat."* Another neighbor, Agnes Puddington then testified that, *"On April eleventh, a little after Sunset, Mrs. Evans and I saw a yellow cat. John then came and also saw the cat that Mrs. Evans said followed her wherever she went. My John tried to shoot the cat, but it got up a tree, and the gun would not take fire. The yellow of the cat vanished away on the plain ground....and Goody Walford then appeared before our eyes, coming from the woods."* The Magistrate of Portsmouth found Jane Walford not guilty, but stories persisted that she roamed the woods and seashore in the form of a cat that varied in colors from yellow, to red, to black. Thirteen years later, she sued one of her accusers, Robert Couch, for slander and won her case receiving five pounds in damages.

A similar case of a witch supposedly turning into a cat, then suing her accuser and winning damages for slander, had taken place in Marblehead, Massachusetts exactly ten years earlier. Jane James, thought by some of her neighbors to be *"a common lyer, a thief, and a false forsworn woman,"* had been found guilty of stealing from Anthony Thatcher's home in 1639. And in 1646 she was before the magistrates again, this time, for disturbing the peace. Thomas Bowen testified that while with William Barber in his house, Jane James entered the house, and Barber ordered her out, shouting, *"get outdoors you filthy old baud."* Bowen said that Barber threatened to *"cuddle her hide,"* and then he picked up a firebrand from the hearth *"and chased her out."* Jane then gave Bowen and Barber *"the evil eye,"* and cursed them. A week later, said Bowen, *"Barber's chimney fell in, a brick barely missing his head,"* the result of a witch's curse on the house. Peter Pitford, another neighbor, testified that *"I seed Jane James in a boat in the harbor, and she did change into a black cat right before my eyes."* Another neighbor, John Gatchell, upset with Jane's loud foul mouth, also said he saw her transform herself into a black cat, and that her screechings at night as a cat were as foul as her speech during the day. Jane's husband, Erasmus James, decided his wife had suffered enough persecution and he sued Gatchell for defamation of his wife's character. Surprisingly, Jane was found not guilty and Erasmus won his counter-suit, receiving fifty shillings per order of the court. Some 46 years later, those accused of witchcraft in Marblehead wouldn't be treated as gently.

During the hysteria of 1692, the young witch-hunters of Salem, went searching in neighboring Marblehead and found good pickings in this isolated fishing village. Old toothless Wilmot *"Mammy"* Reed made no bones about being a witch. She had cursed Mrs. Simms of Salem in front of many witnesses, saying she, *"would never mingere"* (urinate) *"or carcare again,"* and the curse came to pass: Poor Mrs. Simms couldn't urinate or pass a stool until September 22nd of that year, the day Mammy Reed swung from a rope at Salem's Gallows Hill. Once a neighbor of Mammy's, Sam Wardell, a tall, lanky young man of 24, was accused of being a wizard. His crimes were *"loving a gurll of fourteen, but couldn't have her;"* drinking rum, *"but not getting drunk;"* and *"telling fortunes, which sometimes come to pass."* He shared a tree branch with Mammy Reed on September 22, 1692.

One old curser and lover of cats who escaped the gallows was the witch of Sutton, Massachusetts, known as Widow Wakefield. Goody Wakefield lived by the river in a weather-beaten house with twenty cats. She was able to feed herself and her pets by catching pickerel in the river each day. She always wore a heavy coat summer and winter that had large pockets, where she'd keep her daily catch. Neither the evil eye nor the malignant touch was needed by Widow Wakefield to cast a spell, just to walk by her house or to pass her on the road would send one reeling from the smell. In disgust, two young men of Sutton decided that they would attempt to rid the town of the smelly old witch by killing off all her familiars. One night they succeeded in capturing and killing 17 of her cats. They layed their broken bodies out on a rock slab in front of her house so that she would see them the moment she left her home in the morning. Apparently, the youths thought the shock of seeing her pets might kill her, but it didn't. Although devastated, the widow shouted her curse into the wind so her neighbors could hear. *"God, curse these killers,"* she screamed over and over again, and those that heard her were surprised that she had called on God and not the devil. The two young men did indeed feel the effects of the curse, for within the year, one drowned accidentally in the river, and the other contracted a disease that left him a babbling idiot for the rest of his natural life.

Although some accused of being witches in bygone days were described as young and beautiful, most are depicted as old hags with long noses and warts on their faces, much as the typical image of a witch revealed every Halloween. In Colonial days, any woman who reached thirty years of age without getting married, was considered an old maid. John Dunton of Boston writes of a girl just turned *"about thirty, the age which they call a Thornback."* He says that, *"she is an ancient maid, yet she never disguises herself, and talks as little as she thinks of love."* Reverend Higginson of Salem, mentions a girl in his congregation as being *"an old virgin of twenty-five years."* An English visitor to New England during Witch Times, wrote home to say that *"the women here are pitifully tooth-shaken,"* and that, *"several old women suspected of witchcraft in and about Essex, have been noted to have beards of considerable growth."*

Since witches were almost always considered quite old and ugly, no matter what their age might be, many Colonials believed that they would be frightened away if they saw their own image. Yet mirrors, crystal-balls and crystals have always been considered quite magical, even divine, down through the ages. To break a mirror, as we all know, means seven years bad luck, and this derives from our primitive ancestors believing that the image in glass or crystal is really not you, but your soul. If, therefore, you break that image, you lose your soul. It was also believed, well into the eighteenth century, that mirrors like crystal-balls could foretell the future, and to break one would destroy that future. *"Inhabitants of hell cast no reflection,"* was firmly believed by the early Americans, and if the devil or a witch familiar stood in front of a mirror, there would be no reflection. But, a witch who had not yet entered hell, would flee at seeing her haggard self.

Witch-balls of colored glass, looking like crystal-balls, were often hung over doorways or displayed on mantles to protect the home from witches, and these protective glass spheres were displayed in New England homes well into the nineteenth century. Sometimes they were filled with special herbs that witches detested, like ground up poison-ivy leaves, which the witches called "mercury", or sometimes they were filled with blessed holy-water. But whichever, when a witch saw her reflection in the rounded mirror-like glass, she would leave or disappear. These witch-balls are still used for decorations in homes, but most people today don't know what they are or the siginficance of displaying them. Some farmers, I'm told, still hang them in the rafters of barns to protect their livestock from the evil doings of witches.

"I fear some young persons through a vain curiosity to know their future condition, have tampered with devil's tools," said Reverend John Hale in 1692, in his *"Modest Inquiry Into The Nature Of Witchcraft."* Hale was a zealot in ferreting out suspected witches in Beverly, a town bordering Salem, until his wife was accused of witchcraft, and then he moderated his zeal. His wife, it was said, was interested in palmistry and fortune-telling, and a noted Beverly witch Dorcas Hoar, supposedly stole a book on palmistry from Hale's home, making him suspect as well. Hale tells us that he knew an afflicted person who, *"I was informed.... did try with an egg in a glass to find her future husband's calling; till there came up a coffin, that is, a spectre in likeness of a coffin. And she was afterward followed with diabolical molestation to her death; and so dyed a single person. A just warning to others,"* writes the newly converted minister, *"to take heed of handling the devil's weapons lest they got a wound thereby."* Hale thus concluded that the crystal-ball, or glass tumbler with an egg in it, was a devil's weapon. Yet the witch-balls, probably displayed in his own home, were justified.

Goodwife Eunice Cole of Hampton, New Hampshire, found guilty of witchcraft in 1656, was sentenced to a flogging and life imprisonment at Boston Jail. She was then a withered hag in her late seventies. Her husband William, left to fend for himself on their meager farm, was 82 years old. In 1662, William pleaded with the court officials to release his wife, for he could not manage even the daily chores alone. The magistrates refused his request and, two years later, the selectmen of Hampton were arrested by Boston jailer William Salter for not paying the eight pounds per year for Goody Cole's keep that her husband could no longer pay. To avoid arrest, Selectman Marston confiscated the Cole home to pay the bill, and William died shortly thereafter. Goody Cole again petitioned the court for release and this time the magistrates agreed, but only if she'd live outside the court's jurisdiction, which was impossible for her—she was now a feeble, crippled woman in her late eighties. Finally, in 1670, the selectmen of Hampton agreed to give her a shack by the river and have the people of Hampton provide food for her. She was released, delivered back to Hampton, and lived on handouts until October of 1671, when she was again charged with witchcraft. Her crime was that she supposedly cursed the occupants of a boat as it passed by her hut, and the boat soon afterwards wrecked on Rivermouth Rocks, the occupants drowning. John Greenleaf-Whittier wrote a poem about the incident, titled, *"The Wreck of Rivermouth:....*

"Fie on the witch! cried a merry girl
As they rounded the point where Goody Cole
Sat by her door with her wheel atwirl
A bent and blear-eyed poor old soul.

'Oho!' she muttered, 'ye're brave today!
But I hear the little waves laugh and say,
The broth will be cold that waits at home;
For it's one to go, but another to come!'
'She's Cursed,' said the skipper, 'speak her fair:
I'm scary always to see her shake
Her wicked head, with its wild gray hair,
And nose like a hawk, eyes like a snake.'
But merrily still, with laugh an shout,
From Hampton River the boat sailed out.... "

And so, in 1673, old Eunice Cole, well into her nineties, was again facing the Boston magistrates, but surprisingly, the jury found her not guilty of witchcraft. This time the jury did decide, however, that there was *"a vehement suspicion of her having familiarity with the devil."* She sat in jail for two months and then was sent back to Hampton, where relatives and friends of the drowning victims didn't welcome her too warmly. Few now were willing to feed her and she soon died in her hut. Word of her death passed quickly through Hampton, and a mob of men came to carry the body away to a roadside pit where a stake of oak was thrust into her heart, then a horseshoe was tied to the stake, and the body of Goody Cole was set aflame as the citizens of Hampton cheered. Their witch was finally consumed.

The horseshoe tied to the stake impaled in Goody Cole's heart, had meaning—it was to drive away any evil spirits that might still be lingering in her dead body. The lucky horseshoe is still with us today, even though the horse has long ago left the streets. The iron horseshoe like the glass witchball, was hung over doors, not for luck, but to frighten away witches. Witches, so Colonials believed, feared horses, that's why, say some, they rode broomsticks. Legend has it that a blacksmith named Dunstan was approached by the devil to made iron shoes for his own hoofs, but Dunstan tricked the devil and made him an iron chain instead with which he chained the devil to the shop wall. The devil was furious, but Dunstan refused to let him go unless he promised never to enter a building that had a horseshoe hanging over the front door. The devil reluctantly agreed, but insisted that the horseshoe must be nailed pointing up and not down for him to stay away. Blacksmith Dunstan agreed and they shook hands on it, but the blacksmith, later known as Saint Dunstan, still refused to make the devil horseshoes for his hoofs. When the Colts football team was organized, in the late 20th century, the symbol on their helmets was, and still is, the horseshoe. After losing a few professional football games, one wise fan noticed that the horseshoes on the players' helmets were facing down, a symbol of bad luck—and so the helmets were painted over, with the horseshoe pointing up. Although the Colt's haven't won every game since, they have improved.

"Me and Martha Carrier did both ride on a stick when we went to witch meeting at Salem Village," Mary Lacy said at her trial in 1692, and by admitting she was a witch she avoided execution. But Martha Carrier, who insisted she wasn't a witch, was hanged at Gallows Hill. The broomstick had been a mode of transportation for the witch since the 1400's in Europe. Yet Mary Lacy's comment was a revelation to the magistrates and ministers, for it meant that witches could fly from town to town in Essex County in a matter of minutes. The pasture behind Reverend Parris's house at Salem Village, now Danvers, Massachusetts, where witch-sabbats were supposedly held, was a landing-strip for witches on broomsticks to land and takeoff, possibly hundreds of them from as far away as Maine and Connecticut. It was where, Abigail Hobbs said, *"I sold myself to the Old Boy"*—meaning the devil. She said she consumed *"the sacrament of red bread and red wine."* Others testified that at these ceremonial celebrations *"roasts and boiled meat,"* were served and that the meetings were led by *"a tall black man with a high-crowned hat."* Abigail Hobbs, with a wild and lusty imagination, made no qualms about describing the witch meetings at Salem Village and that she *"bargained with the devil,"* while feasting there. Her best friend Lydia Nichols said of Abigail that she was *"a wild irreverent young girl,"* and that *"she lies out at nights in the woods alone."* But Abigail also bargained with the magistrates and ministers by telling these wild stories, and by so doing, escaped the gallows.

The local ministers, of course, were anxious to know who the *"tall black man with the high-crowned hat"* was who led the witch meetings behind Reverend Samuel Parris's house in Salem Village. Sam Parris, a new minister and a recent arrival at Salem from the West Indies, called for a meeting of all the local ministers at his home to discuss this calamity. Among the black-frocked group were John Hale of Beverly and *"a fat redfaced man of conviction,"* Reverend Nicholas Noyes of Salem Towne. It was in the very house where they met, that the terror they faced had only weeks earlier been revealed to them when Tituba, Reverend Parris' black slave woman, bewitched his nine year old daughter and other neighborhood children, sending them into fits and convulsions. After a severe whipping by Reverend Parris, Tituba admitted she was a witch and had *"hurt the children,"* but she also named other Salem women as witches. Like wildfire, the witch hysteria quickly spread throughout Essex County.

Reverend Parris was pleased that he had uncovered this coven of witches in his own backyard, but he feared most the evil leader—the devil's general in the high-crowned hat, who was so bold as to perform his nasty rituals in the pasture and orchard adjoining his own home. *"He must be identified and destroyed,"* said Parris. The answer to Parris's perplexing problem was right across the street from where the ministers were meeting, at the home of Constable Thomas Putnam. His daughter Ann, age 12, one of Tituba's bewitched children knew who this diabolical black man was. Mary Warren, servant girl for the Procters, who also sat around Tituba's kitchen listening to Caribbean voodoo tales, knew who the witch leader was too. *"He grievously affrights me,"* little Ann Putnam finally confided to her minister. *"He choked me and urged me to write in the devil's book,"* she said to Parris. *"He is a minister.... A little black minister that lives in Casco Bay.... He told me his name is George Burroughs."* Mary Warren then testified in court that, *"George Burroughs owns a magic trumpet to call witches to the Sin-Sabbath at the orchard near Salem Village."* Everyone was shocked, but especially the ministers, that one of their own was the villain who perpetrated this nightmarish uprising at Salem. Reverend Burroughs had been the spiritual leader at Salem village in the early 1680's, a Harvard graduate, and presently a Puritan pastor at Wells, Maine. This was a devastating revelation. It was, of course, a lie, premeditated by these hateful and revengeful girls, in a conscious attempt to defrock and condemn a pious man of the cloth. *"But enough,"* cried Cotton Mather from his pulpit in Boston upon hearing the news, *"to fix the character of witch upon him."*

The Essex County Sheriff and his men were sent to Maine to arrest George Burroughs, charging into his home with cuffs and chains just as he sat down for dinner. Burroughs, although slight of build, had the reputation of being an exceedingly strong man. *"He can lift a barrel filled with food and hold it over his head, "* and *"he can hold a heavy fowling-piece at arms-length with but one finger in the gun muzzle,"* were two claims to his physical prowess. And so the sheriff and his men tied him down in a cart during their long journey back to Salem, and still feared that he might break his chains and escape. A severe windstorm arose suddenly during the eighty-mile journey, and the sheriff's men were frightened that it was instigated by Burroughs and his mentor Satan. When they arrived at the Salem Jail, Burroughs was double chained and cuffed hands and feet to a granite wall in the dungeon. His super human strength, Sheriff Corwin and his men decided, was *"the devil's blessing."*

At his examination and trial, seven of the accusing girls confronted him, screaming, muttering, throwing up their hands, swooning, fainting and making many other wild gestures, as if he had brought an army of invisible demons from Maine with him to molest them. Ann Putnam even showed

Judge Hathorne and other members of the court bite-marks on her arm, where, she said, the spectre of George Burroughs had bitten her. Ann's mother accused Burroughs not only of witchcraft, but of murder. He had been married twice and both wives had died; the second, while he was minister at Salem Village, living with John Putnam and his family, Ann Putnam's uncle. *"He hadn't been kind to her,"* Ann's mother testified, and when he left Salem Village in 1683, he had left behind a seven year old waif he had taken in for the Putnams to care for. At the trial, the waif Mercy Lewis, now 17, was his chief accuser. She testified, *"On this May seventh, at evening, I saw the apparition of Mister Burroughs, whom I very well knew, which did grievously torture me and urged me to writ in his book... and he carried me up to an exceedingly high mountain and showed me all the kingdoms of earth. He told me that he would give them all to me if I would write in his devil's book. If I would not, he would throw me down and break my neck. But I told him they were none of his to give, and I would not write if he throwed me down on a hundred pitchforks... He told me he had made Abigail Hobbs a witch and several more...."*

Here was the little orphan child he had saved from the streets of Portland (then Falmouth) condemning him to the gallows, and doing so by twisting biblical stories that he had taught her. A great crowd had gathered at the courthouse to hear the testimony—even New England's most popular and powerful personage was there to listen, Reverend Cotton Mather. Over thirty people, children and adults, testified against Burroughs, including his own brother-in-law, a Mr. Ruck, who intimated that Burroughs could make himself disappear at will. *"He disappeared while we were picking strawberries,"* he said, *"and it terrified me."* Abigail Hobbs, now an admitted witch, confirmed Mercy Lewis's testimony, by telling the magistrates that it was Burroughs who had made her a witch, *"and he brought me puppets to stick pins into."* Burroughs was dumbfounded at the false evidence brought against him. The Bible, which he had spent his lifetime teaching and following, was now being used as a weapon against him—*"Thou shalt not suffer a witch to live,"* was shouted at him from spectators. *"But where is it written that witches have imps sucking on their bodies, and that witches hurt cattle, or can fly in the air?"* Burroughs asked Judge Hathorne, without an answer. Upon leaving the Salem courthouse, Cotton Mather was asked what he thought of the trial. *"It was fair,"* he replied.

Cotton Mather also graced the citizens of Salem with his presence on August 19, 1692, riding a white stallion to the top of Gallows Hill. Following in a horsedrawn cart, hands shackled before them, were four men and a woman, including George Burroughs. The others were: George Jacobs, an old cripple; John Proctor, a hard-working farmer; John Willard, a local constable, who had made the mistake of saying he thought *"the accusers should be punished and not the accused;"* and Martha Carrier, whose children said she was a witch who rode to meetings on the kitchen broom. *"All fire-brands of hell,"* the Reverend Nicholas Noyes informed the large crowd that had gathered to watch. Blindfolded, the five were separately escorted up ladders to the thick branches of trees, where nooses were placed over their heads and tightened to their necks. George Burroughs then recited the Lord's Prayer aloud, *"without a stumble or a stutter,"* one witness reported, and this caused many in the gathering to shout that Burroughs should be freed, for it was understood by all that a witch couldn't say the Lord's Prayer without making a mistake. Cotton Mather, however, calmed their fears that they might be hanging an innocent man. *"The devil is most dangerous,"* he informed them from his white horse, *"when appearing as an angel of light."* With a nod from Mather, the Sheriff then pushed Burroughs off the ladder, and the crowd swooned as he swung to-and-fro over their heads. The bodies of the five were then thrown into a nearby ditch to rot, for it was never allowed to bury witches in cemeteries. The remains of the witches were secretly collected from the ditch a few years later and buried in the basement of a church in Marblehead. One of the corpses, however, was without a head when local merchant Philip English quietly carted them away for proper burial. It is thought that the headless one was George Burroughs. Even after the hangings during Witch Times, there was a rumor going round that Cotton Mather had hired men to go to the ditch at Gallows Hill and chop off the head of Burroughs and bring it to him, so that he might study it.

One superstition from witch-hanging days that persists to this day is never to walk under a ladder. The reason is that when a witch was pushed from the ladder at the gallows, she usually dropped under the ladder, and if you were standing there, this *"fire-brand of hell"* might touch you. It was thought that if a witch touched anything, especially during her last gasp on earth, it would soon die. Therefore, it was believed that if you walked under a ladder leaning on the gallows tree even after the witch had been cut down and disposed of, her curse might still be lingering there, and you would die within a year.

Another popular superstition of Witch Times was that witches made puppets or dolls out of various materials into the likenesses of people they wished to torture or kill. Then they would stick pins into the puppets and the victim would feel the pricks as severe pain, no matter how distant he might be from where the witches performed this evil magic. This was what Abigail Hobbs was referring to when she said that George Burroughs had *"brought me puppets to stick pins into."* Other accused Salem witches, such as Goody Hawkes, her Barbados slave-girl Candy, and Bridget Bishop, all used dolls and puppets to inflict pain on their innocent victims. Judge John Hathorne directed Candy to bring her puppet from Mrs. Hawkes' house into the courthouse. *"It was a strange assortment of articles,"* the court-clerk reported, but mainly *"rags and grass."* Magistrate Hathorne made Candy eat the grass and then the judge himself burned the rags. As this was being done, one of the accusing girls screamed that she was being burned in the hand. When water was used to put out the flames, another of the girls tried to run out of the courtroom to the river, *"as if she would drown herself."*

The Bly brothers, hired to knock down a wall in Bridget Bishop's house, reported to Judge Hathorne, *"we found several puppets made up of rags and hogs' bristles with headless pins in them behind the wall."* Bridget's *"dolls,"* as some of her accusers called them, wore dyed lace dresses, supposedly pieces from real dresses that Bridget snipped from the homes of her victims. A neighbor of hers, Samuel Shattuck, said that Bridget often came to him to have little pieces of cloth dyed various colors, and that Bridget stole money from his home and she *"bewitched my child."* The only cure Shattuck knew to save his sick child was to *"draw blood from the witch's face,"* and dab it onto his child's face. He sent the child with a brave friend to Bridget's house to get some of her blood, but instead, Bridget cuffed the man on the side of the head, and he and the boy retreated in terror. *"This child has been followed with grievous fits since that time,"* reported Shattuck, *"his head and eyes drawn aside as if they would never come to rights again."* Although Bridget said at her trial that she wasn't a witch, and *"don't even know what a witch is,"* she was one of the few accused who obviously had dabbled in the occult and, seemingly, enjoyed her status in the community as someone to be feared. Her bravado, however, led her to the gallows.

Goody Glover of Boston was another who had *"several puppets made of rags and stuffed with goat hairs hidden under her bed."* While she awaited execution in Boston Jail, she was visited by Cotton Mather, and *"against her will, I prayed with her."* Then, says Mather, *"she thanked me with many good words, but I was no sooner out of her sight than she took a stone, a long slender one, and with her finger and spittle, fell to tormenting it."* Spit from a witch, like the kiss of a witch, sucked out a person's soul, so thought the Puritans. It was obvious to Mather that Goody Glover's long slender stone which she spat on, was an idolic symbol of him. He worried about this curse until the day she was hanged.

When Mather's own wife and the wife of the Massachusetts Governor, William Phips, were accused of being witches, the witch hysteria at Salem was abruptly concluded by the governor. He disbanded the witch-court and set free the approximately 160 people awaiting trial or execution. The accusers, most of them servant girls and slaves, had *"done it for sport,"* thoroughly enjoying their one year mastery over their superstitious superiors. In the process, however, they had ruined the lives of many. Even for those who were freed from prison by Governor Phips in early 1693, the stigma of *"witch"* was with them for the rest of their lives and with their families into succeeding generations. The hysteria of 1692 did, however, moderate New Englander's beliefs in an all-powerful devil, and the all-encompassing power of Puritan ministers was also subdued in the years that followed.

Although the Massachusetts General Court did reverse the decisions of the witch-court in 1711, paying the families of the victims at Salem a total of 578 pounds, 12 shillings, the belief in witches persisted. Cotton Mather for one, was convinced that witchcraft flourished in New England, right up until the day of his death, February 13, 1728. In that very year, there was a witch scare in Littleton, Massachusetts, when three young girls convinced residents of the village that an old woman in the woods had bewitched them into taking fits. But before the year was out, one of the girls confessed that it had all been a hoax.

The last trial of record concerning witchcraft in New England was in May of 1878, in of all places, Salem, Massachusetts. Lucretia Brown of Ipswich sued Daniel Spofford of Salem for *"wrongfully and maliciously harming her, with intent to injure, causing her great suffering of body and mind with animal magnetism."* Lucretia's attorney alleged *"maleficia"* of Spofford's ability to control her mind from a distance to *"the power of witches sticking pins in puppets to afflict victims."* Lucretia had suffered *"a temporary suspension of the mind"* whenever Spofford, living some 15 miles away, longed for her. The judge wisely dismissed the case for lack of evidence. Witchcraft was long dead in Salem, but lustful demons, it seems, still filled the air.

Elroy Shaw of Hampton, New Hampshire, draws water from Goody Cole's "Witch Well," located near her home and her grave. Superstition still persists that the water here never goes foul or brackish and has curing qualities for many diseases and ailments.

Nicholas Noyes, Puritan minister at Salem in 1692, stands before the hanging tree at Gallows Hill, where he delights at watching "these firebrands from hell", as he called them, be executed for their supposed sins.
From the television mini-series "Three Sovereigns for Sarah."

III
That Old Black and White Magic

Every race and nationality that came to America contributing to our famed melting-pot, brought with it the superstitions of its ancestors. To the Yankees of New England, the Africans, Irish, Scots, Germans and Italians seemed especially superstitious. And yet, it wasn't long after the new immigrants settled here that the descendents of the first settlers became infatuated with some of their fanatical unfounded beliefs. As poet John Greenleaf Whittier noted of the first mass immigration into Massachusetts and New Hampshire, *"The Irish who settled here about the year 1720, they brought indeed with them, among other strange matters, potatoes and fairies."* The fairies Whittier speaks of, were called by the Irish, *"leprechauns,"* and most Irish, well into the 19th century, believed in their existence. They were devilish little men, tricksters, who could appear and disappear at will, and would reveal to anyone who caught one, the locations of buried crocks of gold. The Scots, distant cousins of the Irish, believed in *"brownies,"* a more subdued version of the leprechaun. Brownies lived in the kitchen fireplace, and belief was that the owners of the house had a responsibility to always keep these fairy-creatures warm by keeping a constant fire in the hearth. The Yankees noted that Scots-Americans, when moving from one house to another, would always remove burning embers from the old house to the new, to provide a warm home for the brownies that would move in right along with the family. This was how the tradition of *"house-warmings"* started, when friends and relatives have a party in the new home for families recently moved from one location to another.

Brownies like leprechauns could be good or evil and most times remained invisible to humans, but once all occupants of a house had gone to bed they would appear and spend the night frolicking in the kitchen. Children and some adults during colonial times swore oaths that they had heard and even had seen fairies at night in the kitchen. The noises were probably from mice and the sightings due to sleepy eyes or hallucinating brains. But nevertheless, the woman of the house was obliged to sweep the kitchen floor first thing in the morning, to rid the house of evil droppings or fairy-dust that the brownies might have left behind the night before. Also, a sharp-edged kitchen-knife with an iron handle was a necessary utensil during the 17th and 18th centuries, not so much for cutting, but for magic protection against evil brownies. If, however, you crossed the iron-handled knife with another knife, the magic that subdued evil brownies was short-circuited and you would absorb the anger of the malicious fairy, destined to quarrel with someone before nightfall. The typical cross made with this knife at the top of bread-loaves before they are placed in the oven, housewives today might think is to help the bread rise, but in early days, it was to allow any evil breath of brownies to escape.

Other quaint superstitions originating from the presence of brownies living in the kitchen have followed us down to this day: If you drop a fork accidentally to the kitchen floor, you will soon have a female visitor; drop a knife, and a male visitor will appear; drop a teaspoon, and a child will enter the kitchen; and drop a tablespoon, and an old person will arrive. Do not throw vegetables into the fireplace, or eggshells, for if you do, the brownies will be upset and cause you and your pets great harm. Brownies are also the reason why so many things are often spilled in the kitchen—for as they skip around the kitchen in invisible form, they are bound to bump into things. The only spilt item that has bad conotations is salt. If salt is spilt, as we all know, some of it must be thrown immediately over the left shoulder or into the fireplace where brownies can lick at it, for they love salt, and for providing them with this treat, they will dissolve your bad luck.

There are many superstitions pertaining to salt that have come to us from beyond the Dark Ages. *"Where salt is abundant,"* went an old saying of the Puritans, *"freedom is as well,"* and New England had its fair share of saltmarshes and salt-flats. Another old belief was that *"if your salt-bowls or shakers are full on November first, you will have peace throughout the year,"* for evil spirits were known to steal salt on Halloween night, and if successful, your home would become sad and its occupants quarrelsome. Scots and Irish-Americans often brought fistfulls of salt to christenings. They would throw it in the air around the room before baptism to frighten off evil spirits that might attempt to enter the innocent child. Old Italian-Americans were known to put salt in the coffin with a dead person as a reminder that the soul is preserved after death. Salt has been a healer and preserver since biblical days and probably long before. It is essential to the diet, was used in pagan sacrifices, and is used to this day in Christian services. It was also once used as money—Roman soldiers were paid with lumps of salt, hence the saying, *"he's worth his salt,"* and it's where we got the word *"salary."* The superstition of spilling salt bringing bad luck, is thought by some to originate from Leonardo DaVinci's painting of the *"Last Supper,"* which shows Judas upsetting the salt-bowl as Jesus says, *"One of you shall betray me!"* The superstition probably originated thousands of years before DaVinci, when salt was more precious than gold and to spill any was a great crime. The ancient celts concocted a salt-brew to purify themselves against evil women (witches), and spilt salt was always thrown over the left shoulder and not the right, for that's where the evil spirit that haunts the mind stood, and the salt momentarily blinded him.

When salt became more plentiful, it was often thrown at newly wedded couples, like confetti or rice is thrown at them after wedding ceremonies today. Its purpose, not only for good luck and a long preserved marriage, but again, to ward off evil spirits that might interfere with their happiness. The word *"confetti"* comes from the Italian *"sweet-meats,"* when sugar and sugared almonds were thrown at the bride and groom—as was rice and wheat—to enhance fertility, both grains being ancient symbols of fertility. It was also thought that evil spirits, always anxious to invade a wedding, wouldn't bother the newlyweds but would content themselves by eating all the rice or wheat that was scattered about.

There is probably not a ceremony today more steeped in superstitious tradition than the wedding. Few brides dare walk down that long aisle without wearing *"something old, something new, something borrowed, something blue,"* and the veil she wears, according to ancient Roman and Greek tradition, protects her from evil spirits. It also is worn over the face as a symbol of submission, for in colonial times a man often captured a girl from her home, throwing a blanket over her or wrapping her in a sheet, and taking her back to his people for the marriage ceremony. The veil, in these supposedly more civilized times, replaces and symbolizes the blanket and sheet. The *"best-man"* originated for no other purpose than to help his friend kidnap the girl of his choice, for some girls didn't go willingly, and often her father and brothers protested vehemently. The best man was there to fight off anyone who would attempt to stop the abduction. Ushers or attendants were instituted only if the potential bride had a large family that would interfere, and then they were called upon, like the best man, to fight off any who pursued the couple. Up until the mid-18th century it was also custom for the best man and ushers to bed down the couple after marriage. They would bring the groom in his nightshirt to the bride's bed and leave him there, but inevitably they would return to the bedroom within ten minutes or so to raise havoc and drink toasts to the couple as they stood around the bed. Judge Sewall, one of the magistrates during Witch Times, wrote in his diary on the night of his wedding, *"no one came to us,"* and apparently he was disappointed.

The *"honeymoon"* originated with the Irish, Scots and Welch, when too many angry fathers complained of their daughters being secretly carted off for marriage. A time of one full cycle of the moon was decided upon when the girl and boy were allowed to remain together alone, eating bread and drinking *"mead"* made from honey. If they still wanted to remain married after that time, her father agreed to consumate the marriage. After the honeymoon, and sometimes before, the girl's father was obliged to present the groom with a dowry of money and precious items, but with the Celts it was cattle, which they considered the most valuable of items. If the potential bride's father had an ugly or for some reason unwanted daughter, he would offer a great expensive dowry to go with her, thereby enticing suitors, and, hopefully, a potential husband. On the other hand, if the father's unmarried daughter was beautiful and sought after, he would demand a dowry, usually of cattle, from the young man who wanted her.

If a couple was to be engaged, the boy would cut a coin in half, keeping one half on his person, and the other half was given to his sweetheart for her to keep. The Welch originated the idea of the boy giving the girl a wooden spoon instead of a half coin, and thus came to us the word *"spooning."* The engagement ring as a symbol of betrothal outdates the half coin and the wooden spoon, coming from ancient Celtic Druids whose power came from the magic circle. Like the American Indians, the Celtics believed that the circle was sacred, and a ring represented permanent and eternal bonding. It was worn on the third finger of the left hand because, it was believed, that finger was attached directly to the heart, and the left hand meant that the woman would obey the more dominant male. After the first marriage ceremony in New England was performed on May 12, 1621 at Plymouth, without a wedding ring, Governor Bradford wrote, *"according to ye laudable custom of ye low countries, it was thought to be most requisite to be performed by the Magistrates, as being a civil thing, upon which many questions about inheritance do depend."* Thomas Morton, however, a constant critic of the Pilgrims, wrote, *"the people of New England held the use of a ring in marriage to be a relique of popery, a diabolical circle for the devil to dance in."*

The bride is supposed to wear white, representing *"joy and purity,"* but even today, that tradition is fading. The groom is not supposed to see his future wife in her bridal dress until the ceremony, for this is considered bad luck for the couple. This superstition originated from the days when parents decided who would marry whom, and the groom sometimes hadn't even seen or met his future bride until the wedding ceremony. It is also customary for the groom to carry his bride over the threshold of their new home, and this superstition again harkens back to the days of witches and evil spirits that it seems were forever trying to get into people's houses. Demons were at the threshold, just waiting for the new bride to stumble, but if the groom carried her, she couldn't stumble, and thereby they avoided the wrath of the evil spirits that lingered at the front door. It was also considered bad luck if anyone but the bride cut the wedding cake. In colonial times, she would cut the cake and then break a piece of it over her new husband's head, and then he would crush his piece of cake over her head. This symbolized the fact that after the evenings activities they would no longer be virgins. It's obvious why this custom died out. Unwedded girls attending the wedding, however, are still urged to sleep with a piece of the wedding cake under their pillow and by so doing, they too will be married soon. Also, the throwing of the bride's bouquet and her garter up into the air for an unmarried maid and gentleman to catch, is still with us, and the ones who snatch each item will be the first in the group of participants to marry.

If the marriage day is sunny, so will be the marriage; but if it rains on the day you wed, the marriage will be stormy. If an uninvited man in uniform comes to your marriage, you will have bad luck; if a horse runs in front of the wedding party, you will have more bad luck; and if a dog shows up during the wedding ceremony, you might as well get divorced right then and there, for things just aren't going to work out. If someone strings shoes to the rear bumper of your vehicle when you depart the wedding celebration, you will have good luck; if you are rubbed or kissed by a cat just before the wedding, you'll have a happy marriage; if a bridesmaid throws away a pin just before the marriage, the couple will be happy forever. The list of bad and good luck superstitions concerning brides and grooms is seemingly endless. The word *"bridal"* comes from the Teutonic word *"to cook,"* and everyone knows that from the wedding day on, the new bride will be a cook. If luck is with the groom, she'll be a good one!

Young people today would scoff or laugh at the superstitions concerning courting and spooning, but many of them were taken quite seriously by our forefathers and mothers. Kissing was actually outlawed in Puritan New England, and kissing in public could get you a day in the stocks, or even a public whipping. The kiss was thought to mix the souls, and therefore was considered quite dangerous. New England Indians didn't even know what a kiss was until the French came to the New World. Indians smelled each other and hugged. The French-Canadians had no qualms about kissing, for to them a kiss was a sign of friendship and also symbolized a contract or an agreement between two people. The Puritans were appalled when they saw two Frenchmen kissing each other in public. The X, which symbolized the kiss, also was used as a signature by the French and the Scots when signing an agreement, for many of them could not read or write in colonial days. The X was first the mark of Saint Andrew and soon came to mean a sacred promise. Many of the first French settlers married Indian girls, whereas the introverted Puritans and Pilgrims shunned such marriages. The English settlers were, it seems, quite shy when it came to courting procedures as, for example, when Miles Standish sent John Alden to Pricilla Mullen's home to tell her that he was interested in dating her, and Priscilla quipped, *"speak for yourself John."* Many people today believe that this was just a cute story about the Pilgrims made up in verse by Longfellow, but it was based on fact, and Priscilla ended up marrying the shy messenger rather than the timid soldier.

That the stork brings babies, (our cowardly way of explaining birth to our children), comes to us from the Germans and Dutch, who emigrated from European environs where storks often nestled on their rooftops. Unfortunately, many young girls in colonial times believed that story until their wedding night. If a child was born dead, or *"still-born,"* as was the term, it was sometimes buried under the front door of the house as a warning to the ever-present demons lingering there. The Irish and Scots also warned pregnant women to keep the baby close to them at all times immediately after birth, for fairies loved to steal newborn babies. Neither the demons at the front door, nor the fairies, it seems, were interested in girl babies—only boys. An added protective device was to wrap the baby in a blanket of blue, for evil spirits feared the color blue. Blue is the color of heaven, and even in the Arab world, front doors are painted blue to close out anything evil that might pass by their homes. Pink blankets and pink clothes are given to girl babies because it is the color of the sweet smelling and beautiful New England pink-rose.

If a newborn boy smiles when he first sees his father, he will become a lawyer or preacher, and it was expected of every Puritan family that the first son become a preacher. If the baby lifts his hands to his father, he will be a leader of men, and if he sneezes, he will become very wealthy. The Scots even had a poem concerning the future of every child born on every day:

> *"Monday's child is fair of face,*
> *Tuesday's child is full of grace,*
> *Wednesday's child is dour and sad,*
> *Thursday's child is merry and glad,*
> *Friday's child is loving and giving,*
> *Saturday's child must work for a living,*
> *And the child that is born on Sabbath Day,*
> *Is wise and bonny, good and gay."*

Since the time of the Middle Ages, the seventh son born to a family, especially if his father was also a seventh son, was not only to have luck in life, but it was thought he possessed miraculous powers. He could see demons lurking about that nobody else could see, and he could subdue them. He also had the gift of healing the sick and the diseased. He was, therefore, predestined to be a doctor. The seventh daughter also, if her father or mother was the seventh offspring in their family as well, had supernatural powers much like a witch, but without any connection with the devil. She could predict the future and was also considered a healer of sick minds, bodies, and souls. In colonial times, the eighth and 15th child born into a family were also considered special. Benjamin Franklin of Boston, born 1706, was his mother's eighth child, and the 15th of his father's 17 children born of two marriages, making Ben especially gifted.

The number seven has always been considered lucky, expecially to gamblers, the seventh horse of the seventh race is always a favorite, just as the number 13 has always been unlucky. The British have tried to pass off fear of the number 13 as pure superstition, until in World war II they could find but few volunteers to man ships and submarines designated as #13. The French, on the other hand, are openly suspicious of that number, and hardly a home in France or French-Canada will be numbered 13 on a street, but will display the number 12½ instead. Many buildings in America do not have 13th floors, and some hotels do not have a number 13 room number. Ships, including modern ocean liners, are often not allowed to leave port by their owners or captains on Friday the 13th. And 13 guests sitting at a dinnertable is still considered unlucky, the belief being that one at the table will die before the year is out. This latter superstition may stem from 13 being present at Christ's last supper. Yet, the pagans, prior to Christ, feared the number 13 as well. The Vikings, before ever hearing of Christ, considered 13 seated at a banquet table an evil omen. In colonial days, bakers, who often tried to cheat the public by raising prices for loaves of bread, had their ears pinned to the pillories, and some were hanged. Thus, good bakers tried to make amends for their untrustworthy peers by giving 13 loaves of bread or cakes for the price of a dozen, known today and then as a *"bakers dozen,"* or a *"devil's dozen."*

Pagans considered Friday a lucky day, for *"the fortunate planet"* Venus influences the world that day. But Christ died on a Friday, and people changed their minds about it, even though the day is called *"Good Friday"*. Actually, Friday and the number 13 should be considered lucky for Americans, especially New Englanders. Columbus sailed from Spain on a Friday and discovered America on a Friday. He first set foot on North American soil on Friday, June 13, 1498. The year before that, John Cabot sighted Newfoundland on a Friday, but his North American discovery never did count because he thought he was in China, so Columbus still gets all the glory. Batholomew Gosnold left England to explore and settle in New England for a few months on Friday, March 6, 1602, and landed at Kennebunk, Maine, on a Friday. Samuel de Champlain left Canada to explore New England on his first of three voyages here on a Friday, two years after Gosnold. On this trip he discovered and named Mount Desert Island in Maine, but he also discovered that the local Indians had long ago named the 13 mile-long island, *"Old-Thirteen,"* because of its thirteen hills. America's thirteen colonies rose up in revolution, its spark ignited here in New England. And when the umbilical cord from England was finally cut, we began building our White House on Friday, October 13, 1792—and we introduced our own anthem, *"The Star Spangled Banner,"* written on Friday, September 13, 1814. Our flag has thirteen stripes and our symbol, the eagle, carries 13 arrows in one claw and an olive-branch with 13 leaves in the other. Fridays and number 13 it seems, have been very lucky for America.

The number three also has much superstition and divine belief surrounding it. *"Three on a match,"* has been unlucky since World War I, when the third doughboy trying to light his cigarette on a burning match at night in the trenches, usually got shot at. Three also stands for fertility and the perfection of man, woman and child. And to New England Indians the number three was sacred, standing for the three worlds of earth, sky and water. The Christian Holy Trinity of Father, Son and Holy Spirit, is also a sacred number in the Hindu and Mohammaden religions. Even pagans considered three a lucky number, often interchanging it with their word for *"tree,"* the oak tree being the most sacred symbol in their world. Celtic Druids believed their magic power came from the oak tree. All their secret and mysterious ceremonies were held in oak groves. The ancient Greeks and Romans revered the number three as well. Their god Neptune, also known as Poseiden, was never depicted without his trident.

"Celtic Druids were known as the wise men of the oak," writes Pliny, the ancient Roman historian, in his *"Encyclopaedic of Natural History." "The Celts held a great feast on the sixth day of every month, where white garbed Druids would climb trees to cut mistletoe with golden sickles and lay the mistletoe on white cloths. Then two white bulls would be sacrificed."* The present custom, that anyone standing under a sprig of mistletoe must accept a kiss, stems from these sacred celebrations of the Druids, when crushed mistletoe leaves were used to ease any and all internal pains. The white berries of mistletoe, however, were used as a poison. In pagan weddings, newlyweds were always forced by friends to kiss under the mistletoe, as single men and women are today, usually at Christmas time. The superstition is that unless the mistletoe that they kissed under is burned to ashes on the twelfth day of Christmas, the couple will never marry. Another pagan ceremony that we have adopted is the rolling of eggs at Easter time. *Easter* was the German goddess of the dawn, and her glory was celebrated in the Spring, *"on the day and night of equal length."* She was considered *"the seed of life,"* and the ritual was to roll eggs over the fields where crops were to be planted, which would spiritually fertilize them. This is the origin of *"Egg-Rolling Contests"* at Easter, the most heralded today being the one on the White House lawn.

The prevailing superstitions to *"knock on wood,"* or *"touch wood,"* also comes to us from the ancient Celtic Druids, who believed that the positive power of the gods was stored in oak trees. When you rap your knuckles on wood after making a statement, you are asking the spirits to assist you in making your statement become a reality. During World War II, when the decisions of Winston Churchill were critical to the welfare of nations, he admitted, *"I rarely like to be any considerable distance from a piece of wood."* In colonial days, some people carried blocks or sticks of wood with them in their travels to knock on or touch if they felt endangered in any way. And toothpicks made from oak trees that had been splintered by a lightning bolt, were in high demand as cure-alls and lucky charms.

Many charms of various materials, or talismans, as they were called, were worn throughout the ages to bring luck or to ward off evil. Glass and various gems were the most popular, worn as necklaces, broaches, amulets, and rings, and probably initiated the reason why people wear jewelry to this day. Bone, periwinkle and shell necklaces were worn by our ancient ancestors, and when New England Indians met the first European explorers, they too wore necklaces and bracelets of bone, sea shells and copper. When the Egyptians made glass, solid glass beads became popular, and blue glass necklaces have been found in ancient tombs dating back to 2,000 B.C. The Babylonians first assigned gems to the planets by color, thereby giving everyone a birthstone, the precious stones providing magical powers to the wearers. The bloodstone supposedly provides courage; the emerald, happiness; the turquoise, success and so on through all twelve.

The diamond, however, although considered *"girl's best friend,"* is one of the few gems that has gained an evil reputation. *The Hope Diamond,* the largest ever to be made into a necklace, is thought to bring death and disaster to any wearer. It is now on display at the Smithsonian Institution, mainly because few women dare string it around their neck. Even a replica that was made of the Hope Diamond, owned by a Hartford, Connecticut jewelry store proprietor, was tossed by him into the Connecticut River in 1962, *"because it is cursed,"* he announced to the press, *"and I don't want anyone else to have the bad luck I've had since I purchased it."* When the river flooded its banks two weeks later, the jewelry store owner blamed it on the curse of the diamond. Most of the owners of the original Hope Diamond, including King Louis XIV, were murdered, executed, died in mysterious accidents or committed suicide. *"Good and bad angels are enabled to enter precious stones,"* wrote noted German physician Rudolph II of Germany in 1609. *"It is more especially pleasing to the spirit of evil,"* he said, *"who steals into the substance of the little gem, and works such wonders by it that some people do not place their trust in God but in the gem... That gems or stones, when applied to the body, exert an action upon it, is so well proven by the experiences of many persons, that anyone who doubts this must be called over-bold...* "Unfortunately, may I be so bold as to say, Rudolph is right, too many people today still believe in the magical powers of these gems. After gazing into any of them for long periods of time, the sparkle may cause partial hypnosis, and this is their real power, not the evil activities of spirits living within them.

There are many other items that are still today considered symbolic of good or bad luck: the four-leafed clover, the shamrock, the rabbit's foot are good luck charms; a broken mirror, touching a frog, or squashing a ladybug, will bring bad luck. A talisman that originated in New England is the turkey wishbone. In our house there are at least two of them drying on the window sill after the Thanksgiving and Christmas day feasts. When the springiness is out of the bone, then two people, each holding an end with the little finger of their right hand, pull until one end snaps off. The person left holding the long piece of wishbone is granted a wish, but the winner can't tell anyone what he wished, or it will not come true. The wishbone was actually a mystery to our forefathers, for nobody seemed to know what the function of the wishbone was when the turkey was alive. Only through the use of X-rays and an air-tunnel have scientists recently discovered that the wishbone helps the turkey breathe while in flight.

If you see three geese flying together, it means you will witness a great disaster, and the Scots believe that encountering three swans swimming in a row in a pond is also a forewarning of disaster. Seeing the first robin of spring, means you'll have a good year. Seeing seagulls flying inland means a storm is coming, and this is more than superstition, for inevitably, gulls will fly for inland shelter many hours before we less gifted humans have any warning of an approaching storm. The gulls are often much more accurate than the local radio and television weathermen. New England farmers, many of them not having the benefit of seagulls in the area, say that a squawking bluejay by the house or barn, is telling you that a storm is approaching. Other feathery forecasters are the owl, peacock, quail and rooster, who announce the coming of storms to humans with a screech, a squawk, a cry and a crow.

New England Indians believed that ravens and blackbirds were messengers from the heavens and would foretell many upcoming events if one would listen closely to their squawking and cawing. New England farmers to this day, will tell you that when chickens start squawking loudly, they're informing you that it's going to rain soon. Chickens, of course, have been forecasting the future and telling fortunes since ancient times, when Pagan high priests would cut them open and spread the innards on the ground as a means of making important decisions. Even today, farmers believe that if the gizzard peels away easily from the skin of a chicken, it will be a mild winter without much snow. In Maine they say that if a man plucks a chicken of all its feathers, he will soon lose all his hair.

A true story that might revive the belief that chickens have magical powers, occurred in June, 1980 at Falmouth, Maine. Ed Robinson, who owns a pet chicken named Randy, experienced a terrible injury in a truck accident in 1972, which left him totally blind and partially deaf. Ed heard old Randy squawking out in the backyard this Summer's evening, and he knew it was Randy's way of telling Ed that a storm was coming. Ed, age 63 and almost as bald as a cue-ball, stumbled his way out into the backyard to catch Randy and bring him indoors before the rain started. Just as he was out the screen door, a bolt of lightning struck Ed on the side of the head, sent him sprawling, and set the grass around him on fire. The shock of it knocked Ed out for a few moments, but when he came to, he not only could hear well, but he could see again. To add to the miracle, hair began growing back on his head!

The rabbit was considered the most intelligent of the wild animals, and it was good luck for a year if one crossed your path from right to left. If you saw one hop into a graveyard, you would be immune to any illness or disease for a year. The legends of *"Brer Rabbit"* epitomized the cleverness of his kind, and it was thought by some that the wisdom of the rabbit was in its feet, especially in its left hind foot. When a rabbit was killed and eaten, the feet were saved for good luck, and many a young boy would carry a rabbit's foot in his pocket to rub when he needed luck and wisdom. This superstition was still in vogue when I was a boy in the 1940's. The rabbit is so prolific that its foot also symbolized fertility, therefore, many older men carried one around, sometimes tied to their belt, for success in their sexual exploits.

Mans' best friend, the dog, also was thought to have magical powers. *"When an old dog barks, she gives counsel,"* was a popular saying in the old days. Dogs have been known to cross America to find their masters who had moved from one coast to the other, or to seek out and find lost members of their human family. Dogs have often wakened their owners when a fire starts in the house, or have howled repeatedly just before or after their master dies. These seemingly psychic skills of dogs prompted the superstition that, *"a howling dog means that someone in the family will soon die."* New Bedford flounder fisherman Bill Montgomery had a strange experience concerning his Irish-setter *"Redsy,"* back in September of 1938. Redsy joined Bill on his fishing boat every day, voyaging out to the banks with him for over eight years and never missing a day, but on the morning of September 21st, Redsy wouldn't budge off the dock. Even when Bill tried to force her aboard, Redsy whimpered then howled and jumped back onto the dock. Bill finally decided it was an omen, and he didn't go fishing that day, thanks to Redsy's persistence. That afternoon the brutal and devastating *"Hurricane Of '38"* slammed the coast without warning, swamping most of the boats in the fishing fleet at the banks and drowning most of the fishermen. Even Bill's boat at dockside was wrecked, and for some unknown reason, Redsy knew all that, hours before it happened.

Animals, and even insects can predict the weather, but you must look and listen carefully for the signs. If a cat scratches its ear, a bad storm is on its way, so believed the Colonials. And if you see a cat licking its claws before breakfast, it will soon rain. If you see a horse yawn, it will rain, and so too, if you hear a mouse squeak. If cows refuse to go to pasture and head for the barn, if donkeys bray, or pigs grunt, all these, so our ancestors believed, meant a brewing storm. It is known that fish swallow pebbles before a storm, and even if you own an aquarium, the fish in it will swallow pebbles before a storm. *"Frogs sing loudest before it rains,"* was a popular expression when I was young, and another was, *"kill a spider and it will rain."* There were also conflicting superstitions concerning spiders; one was *"cobwebs on the hay means a sunny day is on its way;"* and the other was, *"cobwebs on the grass means good weather will pass."* Superstitions of weather forecasting seem endless, and probably the best indicator of an approaching storm is to find a person with arthritis, rheumatism, or an old wound, and if they're in pain, then bad weather is on its way.

If a cow "moos" at midnight or a bat flies into the house, someone in the family, or a close friend, will soon die. If you put shoes on the bed, open an umbrella in the house, bring a shovel into the house, or dream of a white horse, these too mean imminent death to a close friend or relative. Through the ages, horses have been closely connected to death superstitions— if you see two black horses in a row, someone close to you will die within a year, or if a horse interrupts a funeral procession, someone else in the dead man's family will die within three weeks. The reason for this is that not only did many men die in battle on horseback, but warriors were often buried with their horses, the horse being sacrificed at the soldier's gravesite and dropped into the ground with his corpse. The great Indian Chief Blackbird who died in 1800, was buried sitting on his horse. Today in the United States, when a General or a President dies, a riderless horse often leads or follows the funeral procession as an ancient symbol that a courageous warrior has fallen. Sometimes the funeral horse has a black hood over its head, as was the custom when the horse was sacrificed, meaning that the warrior would ride the horse into the next world.

In old New England, not only were the people and the home of the deceased bedecked in black, but all beehives in the neighborhood as well. The youngest child in the family was given the task of going out to the beehives to tell the bees that their master was dead. If this was not done at the funeral, it was firmly believed that another person in the funeral party would soon die. At one such funeral, it's said that as a man named Rogers was laid out in his casket in the house, his grandson was sent to inform the bees in the backyard hive. Soon the house was swarming with bees that settled onto the lid of the casket and remained there quiet for some twenty minutes. Then all flew back to the hive. Mirrors in the house were also draped with black in colonial days or turned around to face the wall, and they could not be righted or exposed again until the corpse was in the grave. The covering or hiding of the mirrors had to be done by the oldest person in the house, for if anyone was allowed to see his or her own image during the funeral, he or she would be the next to die. These duties were never taken lightly.

Even the firing of three volleys over the graves of military men originated as a superstition to frighten away evil spirits; and whistling when you pass a graveyard, which many still do today, was also a way to rid yourself of evil invisible followers who always camped out among the dead. Never eat any fruit or berries growing in a graveyard, was another taboo in colonial times. A superstition I remember as a boy was, *"A broken clock means someone in the family has died."* And a popular song in my youth was *"Grandfather's Clock."* The punchline of the song was, *"and it stopped short, never to go again, when the old man died."*

Some of the superstitions I remember from the 1930's and 40's, believed by most, were quite frightening. If two people in the family, or close friends of the family died within two weeks, then surely a third must die for *"all deaths come in threes."* If a bird tapped at the window and fluttered its wings wildly as if it wanted to come into the house, it meant that a close family member had just died or was about to die, and the bird had specifically been sent to our house from heaven with that message. If a rocking-chair started rocking by itself with nobody sitting in it, my mother assured me that it was a sure sign that someone in the family had died. And to sit in a chair that was rocking by itself, even if another person had got it going, would cause my mother to scream, for whoever sat in a rocking rocking-chair would soon die. Also, hanging anything on a doorknob meant that someone in the house would die within a year. And a pair of shoes placed on a table or bed, would send my mother into panic spasms, for that too, meant death was lurking.

"*If you sing before breakfast, you'll cry before supper,*" was my mother's favorite, and most times it came true. My wife's favorite, which she follows religiously, is passed on from her New Hampshire and Vermont ancestors, "*If you sew on a Sunday, you can't get into heaven until you take out every stitch with your nose.*" Another superstition from the hills is, "*if you sew any article of clothing while a person is still wearing it, a falsehood will be told about you for each stitch.*"

As kids, there were many little sayings that most of us didn't believe, or only slightly believed, but we'd follow the message they provided, just in case the spirits that seemingly prevailed made them reality. One was, "*step on a crack and break your mother's back,*" and another was, "*find a penny and pick it up, so's all the day you'll have good luck.*" In farm country, one was "*bale of hay, bale of hay, make a wish and turn away.*" We were forever wishing on shooting stars and "*star light, star bright, the first star I see tonight, I wish I may, I wish I might, have the wish I wish tonight*" We were also told that we had a free wish coming if we entered a church that we had never been in before, or were first to see a rainbow, or threw a penny down a well. If we lied, our noses would grow, or hair would grow on the bottoms of our feet. If our noses itched, we would kiss a fool or have a fight. Since we boys weren't into kissing, a fight was more probable, and it seemed ironic how many times these silly superstitious predictions would come true. If you talked to yourself, you were told that you had money stashed away, but if your shoes squeaked, you owed money. An itchy palm meant you'd soon receive money, and itchy feet foretold a trip somewhere. If you put your shirt, sweater, or coat on inside-out in the morning, you were told that you must wear it that way all day, or you'll have bad luck. If you and a friend said the same thing at the same time, you'd lock your little fingers together and say together, "*May your wish and mine never be broken.*" But if either of you interrupted this ritual with any other words, the spell would be broken and your wishes wouldn't come true. If you gave anything sharp like a knife to your friend, he had to give you a coin in return or your friendship would soon be cut off. "*Cry on your birthday and you'll cry every day of the year,*" was another one. And if you blew out all the candles on your birthday cake, you were granted a wish; but if you didn't do it with one breath, the magic of the wish evaporated. It was around the time of my eighteenth birthday, when there were just too many candles on the cake to blow out with one breath, that I left behind all these childish superstitions and joined the world of the adults, where superstitions were less frivolous.

A few die-hard superstitions, however, followed me into adulthood, such as stepping in dog mess, or having a bird poop on my head. It's easier to accept them as omens of good luck rather than the misfortunes that they really are. I found it difficult to accept superstitions like getting out of bed on the wrong side making you ill-tempered all day, for the wrong side always seems to mean the left side, and I am left-handed and left-footed. Left, at one time, was considered evil, and in colonial days, left handed children were quickly taught in their first days at school, to write with their right hand and not their left. Left-handed at one time meant *"under-handed,"* and the word *"sinister,"* comes fron the Latin word for *"left."* It was thought in the old days that even if you got out of bed on the right side in the morning, your right foot must be first to hit the floor or you would have a disturbing day. The Puritans also believed that you must always enter a house with your right foot first, or evil would follow you in. The simple act of stumbling, thought to be accidental, was also a warning of a future disturbance or disaster that day. This obviously was a superstition brought to America from England, for Shakespeare wrote, *"For many men that stumble at the threshold, are well foretold that danger lurks therein."*

Other natural, day-to-day occurrences prompted many superstitious reactions from our forefathers, and some of their ill-founded beliefs are still with us today, whereas others died slow natural deaths. Yawning, for example, was considered an evil gesture; some believed it allowed demons to enter the body, and others believed it allowed the soul to leave the body. Colonials used to snap their fingers when they yawned to scare the demons away. And that's the reason why we usually cover our mouths when we unexpectedly yawn, to keep the demons out of our bodies and to keep our souls in. It was thought that sneezing cleared the mind and the nostrils as well. Snuff was popular in the 1700's to induce sneezing. If you sneezed three times in a row, it meant you were in good health, even if you were in bed with a cold. The ancients considered sneezing an evil omen, the closest thing to death; yet, in some cultures, sneezing means good luck. If a Yankee-Doodle-Dandy sneezed while someone was talking, it meant that he wasn't interested in what was being said, much as a yawn today is regarded. It's where we get the expression, *"that's nothing to be sneezed at"*—in other words, what's being said is important.

Spitting has always been considered magical and even sacred by some. Christ, more than once used spittle to heal, *"and he took the blind man. . . and he spat into his eyes."* The Irish still practice spitting into the right hand, then shaking hands, to seal a contract or agreement. And Indians believed that if you spit into a snake's mouth, it wouldn't harm you. A witch's spit, of course, contained a magical curse, but if you could somehow obtain some of her spit (or her urine) you could break her curse and possibly kill the witch. Colonial doctors sometimes spit on their patients especially on a place that was wounded or diseased, for some of these learned men believed spittle and saliva had some magical healing ingredient in it. Even today you might find a few old-timers who *"spit for luck."* Another common yet ancient belief is that when your right ear is itchy or burning, someone is talking well of you; but an itchy or hot left ear, means that someone is talking ill of you. Being left-handed, I often wondered if the opposite is true for lefties. Whichever is true, I think it's obvious that the strange old superstitions of our forefathers, have not yet left us. We still act and react to various omens the way they did, like placing our hand over our mouth when we yawn, without even realizing we're doing it for superstitious reasons. We are still the victims of primitive fears and desires that prompted these superstitions in the first place, and we've replaced a few of the outdated ones with superstitions of our own making. If you think not, try leaving a Chinese restaurant without opening the fortune cookie!

Brownies frolic in a colonial kitchen.

Brownies living in the hearth and leprechauns dwelling neath a thorn-bush, were superstitions that died hard in Scotland, Ireland, and even here in New England. But then again, maybe they weren't superstitions at all—even though you might not believe in them, those leprechauns could be there just the same.
Photo by the author.